DEERLY BELOVED

Deerly Beloved

MORGAN PLANTZ

Made Baugh Us

CONTENTS

~ 1 ~

Special thanks to the most important people in my life, my forever love Timothy, and my four children: Archer, Luna, Leon, and Ruby. Thank you for always pushing me to better myself and to be more than I ever thought I could be. My children and Timothy, my best friend, I wouldn't want to spend this life with anyone else. From I loopy you to I love you, for the rest of my life.

Chapter 1
Wife and Husband

Regina awoke in the morning, bright and early but refused to open her eyes until she knew he was still sleeping. She heard his loud, obnoxious snoring that sounded like a freight train, followed by the long drawn-out pause of his sleep apnea. 10 seconds... 20 seconds... 30 seconds... She always made it a point that if he went 40 seconds before his next breath she would nudge him in the side to remind him to breathe. 36... 37... 38... 39..

The sudden deep breath he took kept him asleep. She was so relieved she wouldn't have to risk waking him up. Her routine was the same every morning. Wake before her husband, make coffee, do her chores, read her book, and get outside to tend to her garden, all before her husband awoke from his slumber. She had loved him all her life as he once loved her many years ago, but alcohol had taken over his life.

He awoke every morning to find her gone from their lumpy bed. He reeked of the previous night's whiskey binge, which caused him to wake up to pour another glass. He was thirsty and dehydrated. His head pounded from the hangover, or maybe it was the withdrawal from the few hours of sleep without drinking. He didn't care. He would roll out of bed, huffing and puffing, skip the shower, and stumble into the kitchen looking to see if she had made breakfast. She used to cook him breakfast every morning. Brew his coffee, and lay in bed for hours. Lately, she has been out to her stupid garden before he ever even woke up.

She would say she was covered in dirt and too busy to be able to cook him anything, and that he slept too long. Instead of food, he would grab his glass and his whiskey cubes and fill it to the brim with Rebel Yell or Larceny. He would take that into his office and stay there for the next several hours.

Her garden was her safe house. There was every-thing you could imagine. Cucumbers, tomatoes, cherry tomatoes, corn, green beans, peppers, zucchini, squash, and surrounding her veggies she had flowers planted all around the plot. Zinnias, marigolds, daisies, azaleas, as well as many other well-loved names. The last thing he did for her before he fell into his alcoholic stupor that has lasted for years, was tilling a huge plot of their yard into the garden of her dreams. Her children were grown and moved out of the house. They used to call every day, then it turned to every other day, now it was only every few months... (When they remember.) They stopped visiting for holidays also. I think they call this "Empty Nest Syn-drome". Whatever it is, it is terrible. Even so, she would always be thankful they got out of the house before the big Stock Market crash of 2020, after the pandemic hit. It was 5 years ago almost to the day. She remembered because they were so excited. Her husband had invested every last penny they had into the stock market at that time. It was up 857%. They made $200,000 in just a few days. The two were on cloud 9.

Jim, her husband, stared at his computer. There were so many pages open in his tab. He hadn't exited out of any for so long. He thought maybe, just maybe, today would be the day his money would climb up out of the deep black hole he had got himself into. Although he thought this every day for the past 5 years, ever since that day he watched his money dwindle to nothing in just a few minutes. He had gotten greedy. Maybe not greedy, maybe had gotten hopeful, he tried to convince himself. Hopeful that he could give his wife the house she always prayed for. The huge piece of land, the cattle, the garden she always longed for. They would have horses and have their grandkids over every weekend at the farm to teach them the values of hard work and responsibility. His wife and he would watch the sunrise and sunset every day and night together on a bench at the top of a hill that he would build with his bare hands. He would paint it her favorite shade of plum purple and engrave their initials inside of a heart. Their grandkids would make handprints in a special concrete circle in the middle of the garden. They were going to be so happy, but the pandemic hit, washing those dreams away in an instant.

It was almost the weekend and she had to hurry and prepare for her big plans. Every Saturday morning she would pack up and go down to the local park to set up her garden and flower stand. She would place her table beside a beautiful prairie filled with wheat grass and wildflowers. The background always looked so pretty with the flower-hanging baskets that she brought with cute wooden buckets full of all of the veggies she had worked so hard to grow and harvest. She was an amazing and classy yet very humble woman of beauty and inspiration. She was working so hard to save up for the brand new GM digital camera with 100 megapixels. It was $5,000 out of pocket. She was sure she would be able to sell her veggies and flowers and make enough to buy it. That was going to be her new happiness. 2025 was going to be her year. She was going to take up photographing wildlife. It would keep her out of the house and be able to relax after working in her garden on hot days. When it is wintertime and too cold for the garden to grow, she could go out into the prairie and photograph. This particular Saturday was a slower day and not many people were out in the park. That gave her a lot of time to think back on everything that had happened...

Chapter 2
Flashback 20/20

It was January 2020, and the news about a suspicious virus was running around the world. There wasn't much panic at the time. Most people thought it was just going to stay in China and not affect the United States. Life was good for most Americans, especially for my husband and me. Our children were eighteen and nineteen years old this month. Proctor, my 19-year-old, wanted to take a year off of school to save money for college, so he stayed at home and started work on a pipeline because he thought that would give him the money he needed in the right amount of time. Chadwick, or as I loved to call him Wicker (he hates that), was turning 18 in just a few days. My last baby, and the most headstrong to leave this town. He had worked multiple odd jobs since he was fourteen to save money. His dream was to go to California and get into an acting career or to be famous, anything to get him out of the house making him better than his father and I.

I met my husband when I was twenty, after two years of college. We were in the same Business Ethics course and he caught my eye, or rather I caught his eye after tripping down the stairs to get to my chair one day (how embarrassing). He had this voice that was kind of southern, kind of city, and kind of everywhere in between. He was older than I was, by ten years. He had traveled the world and wanted a new start. He had lost his passion for adventure. He wanted to settle down and enter the stock market world. He was very intelligent and remarkably good at doing small buys and sells here and there in the market. He was already well off when I met him. Not that the money mattered, I was head over heels for him (literally) since I first met him. He was so sweet. The most gentle and caring person I had ever met. And oh was he funny. No matter what mood I was in, he could get a belly laugh in the middle of me having a mental breakdown over something dumb, like not feeling worthy or good enough for him.

Our first holiday together was Valentine's Day. He despised Hallmark days due to many bad memories with his MANY ex-girlfriends over the years. I loved holidays back then, and I loved gift giving. I expected nothing in return as I knew he didn't care for the day. I had known him only a few days before February 14th, but in that small amount of time, I was able to find the most impeccable gift for him. A Damascus steel pocket knife. It was a four-inch blade with a curved tip. The scales (the handle) were made of Ebony wood that had been stained blue. The swirls of the grain in the wood complimented the whole knife perfectly. He was going to love it. I placed it in a small cardboard box, and wrote a little love note on top, just shy of telling him I loved him so as not to scare him off. The moment he opened the box his face shined with excitement. He said it was absolutely perfect. He put it in his pocket, and he carried it on his person ever since.

That was the night we made our first little boy. He is nineteen now. He worked from sunup to sundown and all hours in between. The pipeline was hard, grueling work, but somehow he always managed to enjoy the physical labor. He was tall and muscular with strong facial structures. He had beautiful, wavy brown hair, just like his daddy. His work made it so he never had time for girls. Wicker on the other hand was just like his daddy, in the girl's way. New gal every other night. He was in his prime and he was blessed with very good genes. I never cared for the number of women he went through, but he was eighteen and it was none of my business. I tried bringing my boys up with the most love and manners I knew.

February came in fast. The stocks were surging, we were making so much money. We were finally making plans to build the home we had been planning since we started dating. It was going to be big and beautiful on twenty acres of land. It was going to be a pole barn house. It was an open concept home with a wrap-around porch, all the way around the barn. He was going to let me completely customize the kitchen and dining areas, while he designed the living area and man cave. Our bedroom we would build together. He would construct a huge garden that we would tend to jointly, with flower beds everywhere along the property. We would have a farm area with a multitude of animals. We would retire happily. But that all changed when March rolled in.

The night before, we had been sitting on our small porch outside of our small cape cod house in town. We were drinking margaritas and observing the rising after-market percentages on our stocks. They just kept climbing. We had accrued quite a bit of money in the few days leading up to that day, so we thought we would be able to increase our amount in our brokerage account some more before we sold. We didn't want to sell our stocks if it was just going to keep climbing. That would have been a lot of money we would have missed out on selling early. Our new property was going to cost a pretty penny. We had raised our boys, lived life, worked hard, and we deserved to be able to retire this way. We hadn't always been the wealthiest of people because, well, kids are expensive. We deserved a break. And this stock rise was going to give it to us. That night we decided not to sell and see what happened the next morning. My husband and I made sweet, passionate love in the small bedroom we had slept in together for all these years. The way he touched me was the most serene feeling. The love flowed out of my lips as he kissed mine. We went to sleep smiling.

We awoke at 8 a.m. the next morning after the premarket opened. There was chatter that something was going to happen that day. All the stocks had comments from people who were worried. Premarket prices were down from the night previous because the big investors were getting scared. When a big shareholder sells their stock, that stock changes pretty dramatically. But when almost all of the wealthy shareholders sell off their shares, that stock plummets. The big boys pull out and then there is no hope for the little guys. Within the next hour and a half, we watched our money go from $200,000 to $18,000. We were in shock. We were speechless. It felt like we had gotten hit by ten freight trains all on the same track, running us over simultaneously. BOOM. BOOM. BOOM. We had already lost so much money that we didn't even pull the last 18g out. There was that glimmer of hope that it would climb back up to where we could make our money back at least some. Boy, were we wrong.

By 10 a.m., our brokerage account read a measly $8,300. We had placed every last penny into our stocks to just get ahead and be able to build our home. Our dreams were crushed in the time it took to take a shower. It felt like walking into an ocean of cold water and walking out covered in fire. My husband wouldn't say a word. He didn't talk. He just stared at his screen showing the market and the account. One single tear was shed. I placed a hand on his shoulder and ran my fingers with my other through his brown, wavy locks of hair. I tried to be positive and hopeful, saying that maybe it will come back up. Perhaps, we can make some of it back after the crash subsided. Maybe the pandemic won't last very long and the market will go back to normal. We just had to be patient. He allowed my hands to stay touching him for a moment, and then he swiped them away, turned, and stared at me straight in the eyes. I saw a deep, black void in them. There was no feeling, no love, no hope. Who knew the night before would be the last time I ever witnessed love from my husband again?

Chapter 3
Leaving the Nest

In the days and weeks that followed, the house was as quiet as a church mouse. There was no conversation, no sounds of televisions blaring, no laughter. There was lingering smoke flowing through the rafters from my husband's cigars. He never ever smoked in the house. Since that day, that was all he had done, sitting in his office with the door slightly cracked so he didn't choke on all the tobacco smoke. The house reeked of whiskey and body odor. He hadn't come out of the room, except to go to the restroom, and those times were few and far between. I would make sure to have a nice hot meal ready at the same exact time every night when I knew the stock market had closed for the evening. He would drag his lifeless body into the kitchen, pause at the counter for a moment, take a deep breath, let out a great sigh, and take his plate back into his office. He wouldn't look at me or talk to me. He was so ashamed that he had ruined everything for us and our future. If only he would talk to me, maybe I could tell him I was only worried about him, and not worried about our life afterward. I was content in the little home we had lived in for so many years. We had raised our children here. I didn't need a fancy new house. I just needed my husband.

My children hadn't been home at all. They declared they couldn't stand to see their father so miserable. It had been two weeks since I had looked at their sweet faces, and I only received a text twice in that time from the boys to tell me they were okay. One morning I woke up to make coffee and breakfast, bright and early, so my sweet love could get something nutritious in his body that wasn't whiskey or cigar smoke. Proctor walked in the front door. He looked across the room and peered into my eyes. I think for a second he saw how worn out I was and worried for everyone and everything and saw a flash of sadness. But I lit up as much as my mind would let me because my boy was home. He came around the counter and took me in his arms. My body went limp for a moment feeling the touch of someone finally taking care of *me*. I am a very strong woman but I was so exhausted and overcome with sadness because nothing I could do could make my best friend in that room any better. Proctor ran his fingers through my mess of hair and kissed the sagging bags under my eyes.

And he said to me, "What's for breakfast, Mommy?"

My nineteen-year-old son had called me Mommy. I hadn't heard that from him since he was probably nine years old. His friends at school had made fun of him for calling me that in front of them, and he never said it since. I encased my arms around him as hard as I could and wept. After a few moments, he lifted my head off his chest, took my hands, and led me over to the kitchen table. He told me he was gonna cook breakfast for me. That was exactly what he did: Eggs, sausage, gravy, and biscuits. He squeezed fresh orange juice out of the fruit I hadn't been able to touch on the counter into a large glass and placed it in front of me. Proctor fanned out a napkin and laid it in my lap. He kissed my forehead and told me he would go take a plate to Dad.

I heard him knock on the door gently. No answer. I heard him bang on the door. No answer. Proctor pushed the door open. The sight of his father brought pain, then anger and sadness, and then back to anger. He let himself go. He was slouched over in his office chair with whiskey spilled down his shirt, a cigar smoking at the very end of it while the ash had fallen onto the table. Proctor slammed a book on his father's desk. He awoke with a jolt and a swing of his fist. Proctor grabbed his arm in mid-air and picked his father up by the collar.

"Get the hell up. NOW. Get your ass in the shower, you smell like absolute shit, and THEN you can have your food," I heard him yell from the office.

"You are done sitting here day after day and sulking in your fluids. You're better than this. You have a wife in the kitchen that absolutely adores you no matter if you're rich or poor. She's going to need you in the coming months. I'm leaving and she is going to be *alone*. Get your shit together, Father".

His father reeled in defeat and disinterest, giving in to the assault, unlike the person he was in the past, allowing no show of heart or concern. I dropped her glass. It shattered to the floor all over her nice rug. I just stood there. Did he mean what she thought he meant? He was...leaving? Like, leaving?

Proctor mumbled heaps of cuss words under his breath as he ran to me. He didn't mean for me to find out that way. He wanted a nice breakfast and to serve his mother in a way that he could thank her for everything she had ever done for him over his 19 years. He knew he wasn't the easiest child to raise. Seeing his father looking like a miserable pig when he had always seen and thought of him as the wisest, most intelligent, hardworking man he had ever known, and had looked up to for so many years... was a punch in the gut. And he was *mad*. Especially because his mother looked so worn and miserable over worrying about his dad, and Proctor and his brother never coming home for weeks. Why hadn't he noticed? How was he going to explain this to his mother now?

His father walked to the bathroom and slammed the door. They heard the shower kick in. Proctor ran over to me and caught me as I fell to my knees. He apologized profusely and managed to get me into my chair. He said he wanted to make sure I was going to eat to keep my strength up as he expounded on the situation. He explained to me that the pipeline was on the move and that everyone was being told they had to travel 3 states away to start on another part of the project. They had a deadline they needed to meet, so moving was the only way. It would take him away for a few years. He had to leave that night.

All I heard was muddle coming out of his mouth as

Proctor explained he was leaving. I just couldn't fathom it. I always knew there would come a day when the boys would leave but actually experiencing it was heartbreaking. I would have to face the coming months and perhaps years with my husband's depression all by myself. At least I might have Wicker. Though he would probably leave too since his brother is leaving the nest. I nibbled at my food as I reflected on what to say. I wanted my son to be happy and that means he would have to leave. I had to be okay with that.

After about 20 minutes, I finally looked up at Proctor and smiled.

> I said, "I love you so very much my son, and I can't wait to see the progress you make in life even if it is from afar. I'm so proud of you, Proctor. Make sure you send me a plethora of photographs in the mail so I always know you're well."

Proctor stood and threw himself into my arms. Even though he knew she was faking being happy for him, she had always put on a strong face being a rock for them all. He just hoped his father could get his life together for his mother's sake. His father walked out of the bathroom smelling fresh as roses. He must have used his mother's soap. Jim told Proctor to come with him outside. Proctor followed him into the backyard. His father stood there a few moments and walked over to the shed and grabbed two shovels.

I watched my husband and my son dig and till the

backyard for over four hours. Jim had told Proctor that before he left that night, they would both leave me with a beautiful sanctuary where I can escape all of the madness of the world. I didn't have to be cooped up with his stench and anger.

Proctor knew I had no money since Jim lost it all to the stock market. He handed me a check for $3,000 to use on everything I would need to fix up this space as my own. He told me to make it my oasis. He looked Jim square in the eye and told him he better not touch this money of his mother's or else he would come back and beat the hell out of him. This money was for his mother's bliss.

The sun was setting. It was almost time for Proctor to leave. He had a train to catch at 9 p.m. I had made a big dinner as a going-away gift to her son. I so hoped Wicker would show but he had been so distant I didn't think he would. Proctor had told me he had been too nervous to tell Wick that he was leaving because he knew his brother would do something crazy and act out. I set out plates and glasses for four people. I asked Proctor to go to his father's office to see if he could get him to come to the table. He stood and disappeared into the room.

Wicker came strolling in the door singing a song. He came over and lifted me up in a hug and gave me a kiss on the cheek. He looked around the table and asked what the big occasion was. As the two came out of the office, Proctor saw Chadwick. Regina and Proctor glanced at each other while Jim stared down at the table. Proctor told Wick he was leaving tonight.

Chadwick was pissed. *How could his brother leave him*

with this mess, he thought. He was not about to stick around this miserable place, no matter if his mother was there or not.

"Mom, I'm leaving also. I won't be back." Chadwick got up and ran out of the house.

I just stared at the door. My whole life was crumbling right under my nose. I lost all hope that night. My heart was more broken than the glass had been on the floor.

At least I would have my oasis now. I would plant every flower and vegetable under the sun and pour my sweat and tears into it. If I died soon this would be my legacy now. This garden will save my marriage. Not today, not tomorrow, but one day.

Chapter 4
Regina, Saturday Stand, Present Day

I was getting my stand all set up for the day. I loved the smell of the prairie in the mornings. I always started by hanging up my baskets on the top hangars. My wave petunias were looking extra long and wavy today. I had petunia baskets on the left and Dahlia baskets on the right. Dahlias were always my favorite flowers. It was the very first flower Jim had ever bought me. I had yellow and purple ones out today. I regularly tried to bring different flowers every weekend so that people could see the beauty in *all* flowers. Maybe they would find a new favorite they hadn't noticed before. Next, I laid out my veggies in different wicker baskets. I had cute little chalkboard signs on each one in colorful chalk. I put on the apron I had made when I started doing the stand that read "Regina Wildflower". I had painted a large sunflower in the middle. Last but not least, was the sign I made all by myself that I was so proud of. If nothing brought me joy anymore, at least I had my Saturdays.

My first customer was a man who visited the stand every Saturday religiously. He would buy just one cucumber and then make small talk for a few minutes and leave. That day I had placed my camera down on the top of my counter because I had seen a Baltimore Oriole family in the grass. I had yet to be able to photograph a bird of that species due to their rarity. The man nodded to the camera and asked me if I took photographs. I stated I loved taking pictures of wildlife and would love to eventually have a gallery of all I had taken. He said he loved taking photographs as well and would love to see my pictures sometime. I blushed as I told him I was married, but I appreciated the conversation. I said I don't even know your name, I know you come by every Saturday to buy a cucumber but that's all. He said his name was Talon, like the claw of a peregrine falcon. I had never heard that as a name before. We talked about photography for a few moments.

"See you later," Talon said.

That few-minute conversation was longer than any conversation I had had with my husband in years. It was nice.

As the day went on, my stand was hopping! I sold so many flowers and vegetables, more than I had sold in one day since I started my stand. I was getting so close to my goal of buying my new camera. Just a few more weeks until I looked down the lens at a new life. I sold out at 5 pm that night. I placed all my baskets together on top of my counter, put my sign in my carry bag, and took everything to my car. I had a nice silver 4-door sedan. The kids were all grown so I didn't need anything big and fancy anymore. It was just big enough for my stand and baskets. I still had some daylight left so I grabbed my camera, placed the strap around my neck, and walked down the path of the prairie.

The birds were chirping loudly, I could hear the sound of the stream trickling over the rocks. It was so peaceful.

There were no cars in the parking lot but mine so I knew the park was empty. People are nice but the sound of only nature and its beauty is a whole other feeling. All of a sudden, I heard a rustling in the tall grass. A buck had peaked its head up and his rack rose high above the top. He was massive. I was gonna get his picture for sure. What a way to end the day! I moved as slowly as I could, raising my camera up to just the right position. The deer was looking straight at me like he was looking straight into my soul. For a second, I just stared right back. He was beautiful, elegant, carefree, the king of the woods. He looked to have lived a life he could be proud of. The sound of a stick breaking rang through the field. The buck took off into the clearing between the trees. I just started snapping pictures. I didn't know if I was going to get my photo because he took off but I was going to try anyway, even if it wasn't that great of a photo. I began running after him, I couldn't let him get away. I knew that would make him run faster but I wasn't thinking. I realized I was never going to find him again so I slowed to a stop in front of the clearing. I shed a tear. I don't know why that made me so sad. Maybe I felt that the life I could have had might have just slipped through the trees. What a photograph that would have been.

There was movement behind a tree. A man stepped out from the shadows. It startled me for a moment, but then I realized it was Talon. It was so odd because I swore everyone was out of the park.

"Woo wee, did you see that hunk of a buck!" he exclaimed. "Did you get a picture?"

I lowered my head and said I didn't think I captured him. At that moment, Talon turned his head to look behind him and whispered to come here because he saw the buck again. For a split second, I had a feeling. One of those feelings in your gut that tells you something isn't a good idea. Stranger danger. I wanted so much to get a photograph of this deer that I let it take over and ignored my gut. Some part of me didn't care about my gut feelings anymore because my life was miserable anyway. How much worse could it get? He grabbed me by the hand and we slinked into the trees.

As I looked around the area there was not an animal in sight. I pulled my hand away and went to open my mouth to say sorry I need to go.

Talon came up behind me and wrapped one hand over my mouth and one hand around my waist. Tight. My heart sank to my feet. I tried to pull away but I was small and weak and he was tall and muscular. He whispered in my ear if I screamed or tried to run he would make me regret it. He inhaled deeply into the nape of my neck. A shock of fear and a shock of something stronger ran through my body. It had been so long since a man had touched me. Why was I feeling this? I wanted to fight, I wanted to run, but deep down there was a small part of me that got turned on by the danger that may ensue. I still should run.

Talon said that we were going to walk to his car like

nothing had happened and get inside of it. I intended to run. I am short and haven't run for years but somehow I was gonna get away. As much sadness as my life had brought me, deep down I couldn't just leave Jim completely. I still had to make sure he ate dinner every night. No one else was going to take care of his sorry ass. I nodded my head to Talon to imply I was ready to walk to his car. He slowly let go of my waist, then my mouth. He took my hand firmly. He said he wasn't just going to let me walk alone. This was gonna be harder than I thought. We started walking and I got an idea. I dropped my camera, and leaned down to pick it up, he let go of my hand, and off I went. I ran and ran and never looked back.

Bam! My face hit the ground ten seconds later. One hundred eighty pounds of man was on top of me. I couldn't inhale. Every time I went to breathe in, his pressure would not allow my lungs to expand. I told him I couldn't breathe. He pressed my face down harder into the dirt.

"I told you not to do it," he spit.

I then felt something on the nape of my back. It was hard. I was thinking to myself it could only be one of two things: throwing me into the ground either turned him on, or it was a gun. I would be an idiot if I thought it was anything else. He told me to get up very slowly as he pushed the end of whatever he was holding deeper into my back. At that point, he pulled me so hard and so fast to his vehicle I was tripping over my own feet. He opened his trunk and threw me in. I saw him lift his hand with the gun above his head, I felt a flash of pain in my eye and everything went black.

Chapter 5
The Bedroom

My eye hurt so bad, that I couldn't even open it. What had happened? I couldn't remember anything. Why did my eye hurt so much? My head felt like there was a cinder block sitting on top of it. I instinctively raised my arm to touch my face and the pain was unbearable. I blacked out again. I don't know how long I was out. I remember it being light out and now it was dark. I slowly opened my eyes but my left one wouldn't open. I figured I should just leave it closed. Obviously, I had fallen and hit it on something. With my good eye, I looked around the room. The only light was coming from the far corner from a nightlight in an outlet. How odd, I don't remember having a night-light in my room. Come to think of it, I never sleep without my side lamp on, so that was weird that it wasn't on. I realized I hadn't moved my other arm yet so I went to scoot myself up into the bed to sit up and I felt it. I was so worried about my eye I hadn't noticed a cuff around my other wrist.

What!? All of a sudden it all came flooding back into my mind all at once. The man, the deer, the thwack, the trunk. A panic attack ensued. I couldn't breathe. I couldn't move, and I was shaking uncontrollably. Tears were streaming down my cheeks so much my pillow case was soaked within seconds. Then I heard footsteps. The beat sounded like a pair of cowboy boots with maybe a spur jingling. I tried to quiet down my sobbing but I couldn't. The footsteps stopped at the door in front of me. The knob turned, and the wooden door swung open. There he stood, right in front of me. His silhouette was so much bigger than what I had remembered it was. *Please don't hurt me any-more*, I said to myself over and over. Maybe if I closed my eyes it would all go away. What a childish thought.

He sat on my bed, leaned over, and turned a lamp on. The brightness hurt my good eye more than the fucked up one from being in the dark so long.

"Hello Sunshine" he whispered.

His hand raised and I flinched. But then he caressed the side of my head with my swollen eye where he had pistol-whipped me.

"That's an awfully nasty bruise you gave yourself, Regina". he scoffed.

I glared at him with furrowed brows, trying so hard to bite my tongue. I was pissed at him for hitting me. Even more, than kidnapping me I think. His hand moved from my eye down my cheek, following my jawline. His index finger moved up my chin and he held it on my bottom lip. He pulled it down slightly just enough for my mouth to open. He did this ever so gently that I almost couldn't imagine this being the same man as earlier.

"I have a confession to make, Regina, can I call you Reggie? Gina? I like Reggie."

"What? Do you think I am a basketball player, you prick?" I retorted.

No one had ever asked me or given me a nickname. The gentle movements and touching of my skin made me squirm a little. *Why am I aroused?*

"My real name isn't Talon. It's Victor. I was preying on you like a Peregrine Falcon and I was gonna swoop you up with the talons on my feet like a tiny minuscule mouse in a field. You shared so much of your life with me, though small things, that painted me just the right picture. Lonely housewife, shitty husband, poor, children that didn't want to be around you anymore. I was just waiting for the right moment, and your little deer escapade was absolutely perfect."

The deer! My camera! I thought to myself. I dropped my camera when I went running away from him. I wonder if he picked it up before he dragged me away. Even more so, I wonder if I had captured that majestic buck with his beautiful headpiece. Even just one photo. Wait, why am I thinking about this right now? Talon, err Victor, must've seen me in lala land also because I felt him grab my hip. So much force behind one hand. He let out a low growl. He started kissing my neck, traveling down my collar bone. His hand on my hip traveled up my shirt, across my belly. I wanted to scream, but something in me said to let it happen. Maybe this wasn't so bad. Perhaps, it was a blessing in disguise. I hadn't been loved in a very long time. Jim used to think I was the most beautiful creature in the world. That was before he turned into the money-hungry man he was now. We both fell into a deep slumber.

I slept the most peaceful sleep I have had in years. Though I was chained to the bed at my ankle, I didn't have to worry about waking up before Jim, and I didn't have to worry about going to take care of my garden. I loved my plants but trying to care for things every single day is sometimes exhausting. I didn't hear Victor anywhere in the house. I wondered if he left to go to work. What does he even do for work? Not important right now. I looked around the room to see if I could find a phone. I bet my sons were worried sick about me. What would Jim be doing right now? The first morning in years he hasn't woken up to hot breakfast from me. Would he call anyone? Would he go looking for me? Would he even know I was missing?

My ankle was connected to the bed near the bottom of the leg of the bed so I scooted my booty off the side, and I meant to gently slide down but it was more of a CLONK right on my butt bones. Ouch! I leaned forward to see if there was any way to get the chain off when I heard footsteps running towards the room I was in. I bet Victor was coming to see if I was okay. The door flew open and he took one look at me and hurled himself towards me. The rage in his eyes was almost terrifying. He grabbed my neck with those muscular hands and pressed it into the floorboards.

"Where do you think you are going?!" he yelled as spit dribbled out of his mouth onto my cheeks. "You will *never* leave here, do you understand? You are *mine*."

The pressure was compressing my airway and I couldn't catch a breath. I wrapped my hands around Victor's and tried to pry his hands off. Maybe then I could explain I wasn't trying to leave.

One hand of his let loose and he raised it into the air and swung down very fast. The sting across my cheek was something I had never felt before. Wetness escaped down my face. I never cry so why would I be crying now? Another drop made its way. I raised my shoulder and swiped my cheek with it and out of the corner of my eye, I saw blood. The wetness was not tears and I wasn't crying. I was bleeding. He had cut right under the bottom of my eye with the ring that was on his pinky finger. I hadn't noticed that before. As I was thinking about the ring, I succumbed to the darkness that was filling my vision.

Chapter 6
Jim

Jim woke up and raised his head off of his keyboard. He had drooled all over the keys and everything was sticky from the whiskey he had drunk the whole day previous. He was starving and ready for a nice hot meal. Maybe today would be the day that stocks rise. Today would be the day that everything turned out okay. He could finally go back to his normal happy self with the beautiful wife he loved so much. But anger and sadness had enveloped him for so long he wouldn't be sure if the change would be overnight or not. Who knew if Regina would even look at him the same? All he had ever seen lately was shame. What even was today? A weekend? Of course, the stock markets weren't open but it wouldn't stop him from watching the aftermarket numbers over the weekend.

He lifted himself out of his seat and stretched his arms and legs. He sighed powerfully. Instead of grabbing the bottle, he walked over to the door that would open into the kitchen and opened it. He had to walk through that room to get to the bathroom anyway so maybe he would change it up this morning. He was actually going to tell his wife good morning. He peered into the area where she usually stood at the stove. It sat empty, nothing on top waiting for him to emerge. No fruit was cut up for him like there was every morning. The kitchen light was still off. He walked over to the window to look in the garden to see if he could see her bent over in her roses trimming them as she did. Still not there. Jim thought about what day it was. It was Sunday, but she didn't do anything on those days. She didn't attend church. Saturdays were the farm markets so she wouldn't be there. She never missed breakfast for him though. He thought it odd.

He looked at the time and decided he had taken too long lolly-gagging about trying to find his wife and drug himself to the bathroom. He smelled his pits while standing at the toilet going piss and realized he definitely needed a shower. Something had to change with the way everything was going, so maybe he could start with a shower and then go try to find his wife. He showered for what seemed like forever until the water ran cold and he was forced to exit. Jim toweled off and went to the bedroom to put some fresh clothing on. His eyes lay on Regina's side of the bed. He realized for a second he didn't think she came to bed last night. There was no indent in the pillow and her side of the bed was still tucked in. He stared for a minute and then shrugged it off. He was getting thirsty and shaky so he traveled back into his office and fell to the bottle once more. If she isn't gonna be in the house today then he would just drink it away.

The alcohol was causing him to have DTs or delirium tremens. They are basically hallucinations caused by too much alcohol. Beyond his computer screen, he saw his two sons playing in their yard. They were young but he couldn't tell just what age they were. Beyond his boys, his wife stood holding a hose, spraying the boys. She was smirking her big, goofy grin, and the boys were cackling and screaming and having such a good time together. Jim saw himself jog past his wife, smacking her tush on his way past her. Regina adored affection from him. His dick just did not work since the stock market crash those years ago. He just wished the money would come. He wanted that money to make his wife happy. He could feel her pulling away. Seems faster and faster every day. The boys thought he was a shit person. Jim had just given up on life. If there was no money, there's just no happiness. It may not be what everyone else thinks but that's what he thought. No way he could change his way of thinking.

Chapter 7
Regina's Apology

My eyes blinked open. My neck was on fire and my head hurt. I blinked away the dark spots that were enveloping my vision. I felt a body beside me, arms wrapped around my body. I turned my head to see Victor in a blissful slumber. He snored ever so slightly, it almost sounded like a cat purring. I needed to use the restroom but I didn't want to wake him. He almost looked sweet laying there huddled up against me. My back started hurting from staying in the same position too long so I attempted to change the way I was laying when his eyes sprung open and he sat up and grabbed me.

"Hold on, hold on!" I yelled as his fists clenched my tiny wrists. "I wasn't trying to get away, I just needed to shift my body," I said.

"After that stunt, you pulled last night I wasn't going to allow you to be left alone" Victor snapped.

"I'm so sorry you thought I was trying to get away, I honestly fell out of bed" I tried to explain to him. "Let me make it up to you somehow, please?" I begged.

His eyes went from angry to calm in the blink of his eye. "I suppose you can make me breakfast," he sighed.

"Do you like biscuits and gravy? I make a killer meal," I told Victor.

I pulled back the covers slightly and noticed my clothes were missing. I was bare ass naked. Victor leered at me from top to bottom and smirked.

"I don't like jeans touching where I sleep," he laughed.

"Can I at least put on a t-shirt or something before we get up? I am cold." I asked him.

"Not a chance, baby," he said quickly.

He unchained me from the bed but kept the cuff around my ankle.

"Don't try anything funny or the next accident is going to be a lot worse," he explained.

I nodded my head and he led me in front of him to the kitchen. It was spacious, way bigger than mine at home. The blinds were open, letting in the glorious sunlight I hadn't seen for a while. The clock read 9:48 a.m. I can't believe I was out that long. Victor pushed me along until we reached the countertops. He thrust me into the granite with his pelvis and his arm slipped under mine. In one steadfast movement, he twisted my arm in a lock and brought me down onto the counter, my bare breasts pressing into the cold stone. I gasped loudly from the shock at the same time feeling his fingers between my thighs. His wrists forced my legs apart and I was so wet from what was happening, that his fingers slipped right into the warmth of me. I heard that low growl of his again.

A few minutes of heavy petting later, he removed his fingers and chained me up to the counter. He had drilled an anchor of sorts to the bottom. Either this was a very planned kidnapping or he did it while I was knocked out. I wonder if there are more around here. Where are your spices and things? I asked as I opened a cupboard.

"Get yourself well acquainted with the kitchen as that is where you are going to be spending most of your time now. That and the bedroom" Victor winked at me with his smirk on his lips.

He was definitely intriguing.

"I have work to do so don't make any noise so I can concentrate. That food better not take long because I get hangry when I am hungry." He went to another room and brought back a laptop and quite a few files.

I searched through the cabinets and found the skillet and the cookie sheet. I opened the fridge to see a massive amount of food. The freezer was the same. Almost like he wouldn't have to go to the store for a long while. I pulled out the sausage flat and placed it on the counter.

I tore open the package and dropped it into the skillet and cranked the heat up to an 8. That should fry up the sausage pretty quick.

"Could you be a little fucking quieter? He snapped at me. I wasn't aware I was making that much noise.

"I am sorry Victor, yes I will try to be quieter." His hands went back to typing on his computer.

I looked over and saw he had on a pair of reading glasses and was intently working on whatever he was working on when I asked him a question.

"So what exactly do you do? Like, as a job?" I swear his face turned to beat red at the remark and he came rushing over in a rage.

"I thought I told you to be quiet while I worked!" He yelled at me.

I started apologizing profusely not knowing he was going to react the way he did. Mark that down in my head as part of the many things not to do again.

I must have been thinking to myself too much because I didn't hear him speaking to me and that made everything worse. He grabbed my wrist and held the top of my hand firmly down onto the piping hot skillet, scalding my skin. I had had a tattoo there from long ago of a turtle dove but after being cooked onto the skillet it wasn't much of a dove at all. I screamed in pain but only for a second as his other hand grasped my mouth and nose shut. I couldn't breathe, I couldn't scream, all I could do was cry silently. He yanked my hand away from the skillet and demanded I run it under cold water. I couldn't quite think straight from the pain dispersing from my hand so he pushed me over to the sink and turned the water on.

"When I say quiet, I mean quiet, do you understand me, woman?" He asked harshly.

I nodded as tears ran down my face.

"You better respond better than that you disrespectful bitch." "Yes sir" I was able to spout out.

What had come over him? He was being so very sweet and responsive to my body and then all of a sudden snapped into a maniac. He walked swiftly out of the room into the bathroom where he grabbed a first aid kit. He removed a roll of bandages and ran them under cold water. He wrapped my hand ever so gently up in the damp cloth and then wrapped a dry bandage around it. Totally unexpected, Victor wrapped his palms around my jawline and pulled my face in for one of the MOST passionate kisses I had ever experienced in my life. I flinched for a second and then gave in to the temptation.

"Don't ever go against my wishes, okay? I don't

like hurting you but I also don't like to be disrespected. You will learn in time to obey everything I say, understand?"

The look in his eye was so different from anything I had ever seen before.

"Yes sir". I spewed right away.

For the next 45 minutes, I stayed completely silent. I wanted to cry so bad from the pain in my hand but I couldn't. I was so scared I would accidentally drop something. I very slowly broke the sausage up while I added salt, pepper, paprika, and sage to the meat. I had found paprika to be the secret ingredient when making biscuits and gravy. Just gave it that final tie-in taste. When the sausage was browned, I drained the grease into a red solo cup and placed the skillet back on the burner. I sprinkled a cup of flour and stirred it in and let it cook for 2 minutes. I took a tablespoon of butter and melted it into the sausage. From there, I added 3 and a half cups of milk and sprinkled some more sage all around it. I brought it to a boil and lowered the heat to 5, placed the lid on with it, cracked open a small amount, and let it simmer for 10 minutes while the milk thickened up into a nice, warm, delicious gravy. Meanwhile, I made sure to cook my biscuits at the same time so they all would get done at the same time. I set the timer but quickly shut it off due to the fact that I did NOT want that buzzer going off and throwing Victor into a hail storm again.

I stared at the clock for 10 minutes making sure I didn't overcook anything since I didn't have the timer. Once done, I grabbed 2 plates and loaded them up with hopefully the best biscuits and gravy he had ever had. Maybe that would make up for making noise earlier. I walked Victor's plate over to the table and stood as still as possible away from him so that he didn't think I was eavesdropping. All of a sudden he slammed his laptop shut and placed it on the seat next to him. Victor shuffled his papers into a neat pile and placed them on top of his computer, and waited.

"What are you waiting for?" he asked me.

I hurriedly placed his plate in front of him along with a napkin and a fork. He grabbed my wrist and asked me if it was hurting. I lied and said it wasn't even though I thought for sure I was going to pass out from the pain soon. I was starving but I wasn't sure if I could hold all that food down. Victor ushered me to the seat across from him and told me to bring my plate over and start eating. Thankfully my chain reached that far. I wanted to ask if these chains were necessary but that seemed like a bad idea due to what happened earlier. We ate in silence.

Victor finished his plate and laid his fork to the side. He folded his hands and placed them on the table and stared at me. I thought maybe I was in trouble again so I tensed my body and placed my burned hand into my lap for safe keeping.

Chapter 8
The Infection

Over the next few days, the pain in my hand worsened. I tried to keep it clean and Victor tried to keep the bandages stocked, but the blisters started oozing and popping, and soon an infection set in. It started out as my hand was warm to the touch and my whole hand was swollen. I told Victor I thought it was festering but he said we just had to keep trying to stop it from getting worse. I noticed red lines starting to travel up my arm and I developed a fever.

"Victor, I think something is wrong," I told him while panting.

"I need to get you to the hospital, I can't lose you." He exclaimed.

He grabbed the keys and then grabbed my throat.

"Don't you say ANYTHING to ANYONE about how this happened. Definitely do NOT tell anyone who you are. We will come up with a name."

My fever was so high I just nodded my head but that made me shaky. He kissed me passionately and told me he was going to get me well again.

We made it to the hospital in a very short amount of time. That must mean we are somewhere near the city depending on which hospital we are even at. Frankly, I am not even worried about having been kidnapped right now. I feel like I am about to fucking die. He picked me up into his arms and carried me into the emergency room. Victor wasn't taking any shit at that moment and the nurses tried to tell him he had to wait his turn. He told them he would sue them for every dime if they didn't take a look at me. They ran to grab a wheelchair and took me right into a room. Victor was right beside me the whole time. The nurse asked him if he could fill out the forms and he told them we had forgotten our ID and insurance because he was so worried I was going to die. They said they would try to make an exception but the paperwork would have to be filled out soon.

The nurses unwrapped my hand and they immediately stepped back. They raised their hands to their mouths and their eyes were wide.

"Somebody get a doctor in here now!" one of them hollered.

They started an IV and apparently ran fluids wide open because the infection was so bad and traveling up my arm into my veins. The doctor came in and asked how I hurt my hand.

I couldn't really talk so I grabbed Vic's hand and muttered "ask him please."

Vic explained that I had not been paying attention while cooking breakfast yesterday and accidentally touched my hand to the skillet. He told them that I was too stubborn to go to the doctor and wanted to wait it out. He said I ran it under cold water and it started to blister up and we couldn't keep up with all the oozing and had to come in. The wound was so nasty they pretty much believed the story. Granted this happened over a week ago and Victor didn't want to take me to the hospital because he thought I might blab.

The doctor said I would need a long stretch of anti-biotics and my hand was debrided. They never asked for my name because of how crazy the hospital room had gotten when they took off the bandage. The doctor sent me home with a bunch of medicine that ended in -cillins, though I can't recall what all they were. I felt a lot better after all the fluids they pushed and they gave me some-thing for the pain. I asked them if I could leave now and they stated they wanted to keep me for a while longer but I just wanted to get out of there. I signed an AMA form and Vic and I walked out of the door. I think I heard someone say I didn't sign the forms with the insurance information but thankfully we had parked right at the front doors and got out of there fast.

When we were a block away, Vic placed a bandana around my eyes and told me I was not allowed to know where the house was in case I decided to flee. I leaned my seat back and closed my eyes to try to take a nap. I awoke in bed chained back up to the post. He still didn't trust me even after the hospital visit. I didn't care at the moment because I felt like I had gotten hit by a dump truck. I just decided to close my eyes again and try to sleep life away.

Chapter 9
The Boys

Proctor had been working hard on the pipeline since he left a few months ago. He really tried to contact his mother but life was just too hectic. It had been weeks since he had even attempted to text her. He was on his lunch break, so he pulled his phone out. He scrolled down to *Mom* on his phone and pressed the green call button. Proctor's phone rang and rang and rang. On the other end of the line, the answering machine played his mother's voice

"Hi, you have reached Regina. I am probably out tending my garden or at my vegetable stand, but I will call you back as soon as I can, thanks! And if this is one of my amazing sons, Proctor or Chadwick, just know I love you so much!".

BEEP. He thought that was so odd. Mom always picked up his phone calls no matter what time. Maybe he would try again later.

Hours went by while he worked his ass off hauling all of this piping. It was such hard labor, but the pay was making his pockets heavy. He was NOT going to be like his piece of a shit father who sits on his ass all day drinking his life away because of his idiotic decisions to buy a bunch of stocks that went to shit. Proctor tried his mom again and this time it went straight to voicemail. Her phone battery must have died, though she never turns her phone off and she is never away long enough to even get her battery down halfway. He called up his brother Chadwick to see if he had heard from her and when.

"Go for Chad" Proctor heard across the lines.

"Uh hey, it's your brother. Have you heard from Mother recently? Asked proctor.

"Nope not for a few weeks, you know I am busy doing my own thing brother." Chadwick retorted. Proctor explained that he had tried to call his mother multiple times and she isn't answering.

"You are closer, Wicker, can you go check up on her?" he asked.

"No, I am not going over to that house so I can smell our sperm donor for the next mile and a half." Chad snapped and then hung up his phone.

Proctor decided it was time to call his father. Who knew if he was asleep or drunk or both? He dialed his number because he refused to save his number on his phone due to being too ashamed of his father. The phone rang and rang and rang. His voicemail was not set up at all because he was afraid that creditors would call or the IRS would be biting at his phone line. Proctor called again and again until finally on the 5th time trying to call he heard his father's voice.

"Hello? Who is this?" asked Jim.

"It's your son, dad," Proctor answered.

"What do I owe this pleasure?" Jim was confused about why his son would be calling.

"Can I talk to Mom?" asked his son.

"Haven't seen her in over a week. Pretty sure she left me."

There was quiet on the other end. Proctor wasn't at all shocked over that sentence. Something still felt off though. Why would his mother ignore his phone calls? Maybe she was living her best life finally and not being chained to Jim anymore. Good for her, he thought to himself.

Jim was just trying to move on with his life after Regina left him. He couldn't quite believe she would leave without a note or saying goodbye. He also couldn't believe she would just leave her garden unattended and not taken care of. That garden was her safe place. In her absence, Jim had done something that she probably wouldn't have ever seen him do, at least not in a very, very long time. He put his own pity party aside. He awoke every morning at sunrise just to water his wife's flowers and vegetables so that they wouldn't die while she was gone. He enjoyed the small amount of time he spent in the garden while he watered it. It was almost peaceful. No wonder she spent so much time here.

A car pulled into the drive. The door opened and out stepped an older woman, probably mid 70's. She leaned back into her car for a second and pulled something black-out. It looked like a strap was hanging from it.

"Hello, are you Regina's husband Jim?" She called from the drive.

Jim wiped his hands on his pants to get the dirt from the plants off.

"Yes ma'am, may I ask why you are here?" He replied.

"Regina didn't show up at her stall in the park this week and I found her camera laying in the grass.

She loves this camera too much to have just dropped and left it." She explained.

Jim saw her camera and he immediately knew something had to have been wrong. She definitely wouldn't have just left her camera. And she definitely wouldn't have missed her veggie and flower stand. That was the highlight of her week. Jim thanked the woman for bringing her camera back and sent her back down the drive.

Jim went inside the house and grabbed the phone. He dialed Proctor and he answered on the first ring.

"Proctor." Jim paused before he said another word, trying to figure out how to tell his son. "I think something has happened to your mother." Jim finished.

"I'm on my way," Proctor said firmly and with a small crack in his voice.

He was trying to be brave but he was now sure something bad had happened.

Chapter 10
Unchained

A month went by after the hospital visit. I took all of the medications I needed to get rid of the infection in my hand. Victor made sure my bandages were changed and ointment put on. His anger was so much better during this time. He made every meal. I just had to make sure I was always quiet while he was working. I stayed in my room chained to my bed for the whole month. Vic slept with me every night, but the more I spent time with him the more I started to miss Jim. Jim was my person. We made a life together and made 2 beautiful children. I missed my boys so much. Proctor's birthday was this month. It will be the first birthday I have never been able to hug him or tell him how proud I am of him. I had to do something soon. There was no way I was going to miss his birthday. I laid there in bed after breakfast and tried to think of ideas even if it was just to make a call. I made a plan, and it was a great plan.

I would start by making Victor think I loved him. That seems to be what he was all about. He just wanted someone to love him. He seems so secluded and never leaves his house and I have never heard him talk to anyone. He has never talked about family or children or any girlfriend or wife. The first step of the plan is to get him to unchain me from the bed. I took my shirt and bra off and I called him into the bedroom.

"Vic, can you come here please?" I gently said

through the door in case he was working on his computer.

Apparently, he was because he came flying through the door in a rage.

"I told you to be quiet while I worked..." he stopped yelling when he saw me.

I was laying on my side with my top half naked. I had my leg with the chains raised with my foot resting on my other leg. One arm under my head resting and I had my hand trailing up and down my chest slowly. He threw off his clothes in a hurry and climbed into the bed.

"This is different," he said with a heavy breath.

"I just wanted to show you how much I have appreciated you taking care of me all this time since I hurt my hand," I said quietly as I kissed his neck.

I climbed on top of him far enough so that my chains would pull tight and maybe he would be so excited that he would take them off. I pulled my leg a few times so they made a noise.

"Let me pleasure you today, dear," I whispered in his ear. "Maybe you can take the chains off so I can do what I do best." I winked at him while I coaxed his hand down my leg to the chain.

"I don't think so, what if you try to run off?" He replied as he grabbed my throat with just enough pressure but not to hurt me.

I gasped in some air but I was not going to back down. I started kissing his chest and went south down to his rock-hard dick.

"Do me this favor and I will do whatever you ask" I said as I slowly licked from the base of his penis to the tip.

He let out a loud moan, picked me up, and shoved me into the bed on my back. He quickly jumped out of the bed and grabbed his pants. He pulled the key out and unlocked the cold, hard, ring that had squeezed my ankle and cut me like a knife for over a month. My ankle was dark and bruised. It was scarred and cut from the wear and tear of the same movements in that bed. He laid back down.

I was unchained, and I was going to keep it that way. I was going to wear him out so much that he would fall asleep like he did every time we fucked and I was going to make a run for it. I gave the best blow job to Vic that I had ever given to Jim. Back in our younger days, I was a great lover of the bedroom. Though this made me sick to my stomach, I had to do what was necessary to get back home to my family. I rode him like I was riding Jim. It lasted a good hour. Hot and sweaty, Victor moaned and groaned and came and came. He passed out into a sexual dreamland and forgot that I was unchained. I laid there beside him slowly inching my way to the edge of the bed. His hand was wrapped around my wrist as he slept.

I used my foot to bring his jeans up to my hand. I reached into the pocket and grabbed his ring of keys. I had seen Vic pull them out a few times because the inside of the door was bolted 4 times and he had to unlock them in order to go outside the very few times he would leave. This was going to be my only shot at getting out. I realized I had no idea where I was even because he had always covered my eyes with a bandana so I couldn't see. He purposely drove in circles the day we came back from the hospital so I in no way could figure out where we were. I needed his phone.

I managed to get my wrist out of his grasp when I was slinking out of bed. I had rolled the blanket to the width of my wrist and slipped it into his hand as I slipped my hand out of his. I reached back into his pocket and pulled his phone out. I went to unlock it and found the phone was unlocked with his fingerprint. Shit. I looked at both of Victor's hands to see if there was any way I could unlock this phone without waking him. I went in for the "kill". I gently pressed a loose finger into the pad. He started to move and awaken, so I gently caressed his hand that I had touched his phone with and kissed his forehead. He moaned quietly and went back to snoring. That was a close one. I grabbed my shirt and jeans that were laying beside the bed.

I hurried out of the room into the kitchen. I had everything I needed to get away. I started unlatching the door locks one by one. Each one seemed louder than the previous one. After the last lock, I opened the door. The blast of fresh air was overwhelming. I slowly shut the door and walked away. I immediately started running. I didn't know where I was going but I just had to get away from this house and that man. I noticed I was surrounded by trees and bushes. I must be in a forest. When I thought I was safe, I slowed to a stop. Out of breath, I looked down at the phone. Thankfully it was still unlocked. I dialed Proctor's number. It rang and rang and rang. "Please pick up son." I thought to myself with tears in my eyes. Voicemail. I started sobbing into the phone. BEEP.

"Proctor. Proctor, it's your mother. I don't know where I am but I need help. I'm in some type of woods. I think it's near a hospital. Please. Please help me. I love you so much and tell your dad and Wicker I love them so much also. Please."

Chapter 11
Missing Person

During the month of Regina's recovery from the infection, the boys and Jim decided something had happened to her, and they went to the police. From the police's point of view, Regina had gotten tired of dealing with life and she just ran off. Her home life was in shambles, bills were piled up, and no way out of it. It was a small town so everyone knew of Jim's stock demise. Regina was also a big staple in the community with her flower and veggie stand on Saturdays and as much as she didn't like talking about her home life, it always came up with the locals. Proctor and Jim told the police there was no way she would have just up and left. She left her garden she loved so much, she left her sons, and she left her home. No matter what she was going through, Regina never gave up and never gave in. She was too proud. Despite everything, she loved Jim more than anything in this world besides her sons. The police put in a missing person report but that was where it really ended. They weren't going to pursue it. All Proctor and Jim could do was go home and try to figure out where to go from there. They had nothing to go on and no actual proof she was missing. They only had her camera.

Proctor was hard at work on the pipeline. He was hot and sweaty and dirty. His muscles had become very prominent and he was very masculine now. A lot different than when he started his new job here. Though his mother was on his mind, his work was very demanding. He got very few breaks and they were short with just enough time to scarf down his cold meat sandwich and a bag of chips. It had been 3 weeks since they filed the missing person report and every few days Proctor would call to check in on it. Still, nothing had popped up on their radar.

As soon as his next break started, he decided to check his phone real quick. Not that anyone ever called him or talked to him, but he had a funny feeling in the pit of his stomach. With his momma on his mind, he unlocked his phone just to see a message that showed "1 new voice-mail". Proctor's blood started pumping hot through his veins. His heart beat rose so fast, that his hands and feet started tingling. Was this what he was sensing all day? He pressed the play button and listened.

He went white as a ghost as he listened to his mother's pleading on the other end. The way she said I love you Proctor sounded like she was never going to see him again. Proctor immediately called his father.

"Dad, I am flying out to you right now. I just got a voicemail from Mom. She's in trouble" and he hung up.

He had to get to the airport as soon as he could. On the way, he called Chadwick.

"Go for Chad" he heard on the other line.

"Chadwick, get to dad's house as fast as you can. I just got a voicemail from Mom and she is in trouble." Proctor hung up the phone and sped down the road.

Jim dropped the phone from his hands and it hit the floor with a bang. What kind of trouble was she in? So she hadn't left him after all? He ran to the shower to rinse off the despair he was living in this whole time his wife was gone. If he was going to find her, he was going to be clean. He was no longer going to be sulking in his own filth day in and day out and taking advantage of Regina he had done so many days before. As he waited for Proctor to arrive which would take a few hours because he was states away, he looked around at the house. It was a mess. No one to keep it tidy. The only thing that hadn't gone to shit was the garden. He made sure the one thing he did was keep it growing in hopes Regina would come home from wherever she had gone and see the garden thriving still. He was not going to let that die. The garden to him was the equivalent of the love he felt for her all these years in one place. Though he sucked at showing it, perhaps she would realize it after all this time. He wasn't looking for gratitude, he was looking to show her love again.

Because he had some time to kill, he went to his computer to make one last ditch effort to save their finances. He had been watching multiple stocks to see if any would take off. He had a few ticker symbols saved that seemed optimistic. He took the little money he had left from his last major run on stocks and put it all in. It was all or nothing now. He turned his computer off and walked out of the room. Jim proceeded to do all the dishes and sweep the floors. He threw the dirty clothes in the washer and sprayed disinfectant on the counters. He had never bothered to help Regina clean up and he saw how much she was needed, by him and by their home. Jim was nothing without his Regina. He grabbed a vase and filled it with water. Then he went out to the garden and picked a few of Regina's favorite flowers, and placed them in the water.

Chadwick walked through the door.

"Do you know what all this is about, Jim?" Chad said to him.

He never called him his dad anymore. Jim felt so defeated with everything. He knew he was a piece of shit and he was going to change it, and change it now.

"Chad, son, I am going to be better. I know I have made your mother miserable, and I am so very sorry for that." Jim started to tear up.

Chad had never seen his "sperm donor" cry. Jim fell to his knees at his son's feet.

"Please, forgive me. I really do love you so much and I am very proud of you." Jim sobbed to his son.

Chadwick stared at Jim for a few moments. He could see how hurt he was.

"Get on your feet." Chadwick sternly stated.

Jim stood up with his head hung low. Chad grabbed Jim's cheeks in his hands and made him look up at him.

"I forgive you. Dad."

Jim started crying harder. He was letting out so much pain he had been feeling for months that he could never release. Chad hugged his father tightly.

Jim got an idea. Proctor had helped Jim build Regina's garden, so he asked Chadwick for help with another project.

"Chad, can you help me build and paint a bench to put on top of the hill? Jim asked. "She always told me she wanted a purple bench right on top of the hill so we could sit out there and watch the sun rise and fall together."

Chadwick didn't think twice. He told Jim to come on and they went out to Jim's workshop to build. After an hour and a half, they had a fully built bench, big enough for two. It was painted a plum purple. Chadwick and Jim carried the bench up the hill and placed it in the perfect spot.

"One more thing," Jim told Chadwick.

Jim pulled out his pocket knife that Regina had gifted him for Valentine's Day one year and carved a heart with the initials "J & R" into the middle of the backrest. Jim gave Chadwick the biggest hug he had ever given his son and thanked him. They heard a car pull into the drive and they ran down to meet it. It had to be Proctor.

Chapter 12
The Aftermath of the Escape

I had been wandering around the woods for what seemed like hours. I couldn't figure out if I was going in circles or not. I couldn't hear any cars or sounds besides wolves howling and owls hooting. It was a cloudy night so only a brim of moonlight showed down through the trees. I was so exhausted and my legs couldn't walk any-more. I found a thick brush and curled up inside of it and fell asleep.

Light shined through the thicket. It was so bright it startled me awake. First thought was how cold I was. I had no shoes or socks on. I had only grabbed what I could pick up quickly. My hand was aching. I was in such a rush that I didn't grab any of the pain medications or salve for my healing wound. I paused to see if I could hear anything. I was hoping to hear a passing car or some resemblance of civilization. Nothing. I crawled out of the brush pile I had slept in and looked around. Being daytime it was much easier to see my surroundings. I was never good with directions. Jim would always get angry with me because I would get lost just going to the post office and back. I was getting older and my brain was getting weaker. I was not as smart as I used to be. My memory was lagging. I was so worn down.

I looked at the sun and found which way was East. The sun always rises in the east so maybe if I just started walking I could eventually find something or someone. It felt like miles. My feet were bleeding from stepping on all of the pine needles on the forest floor. I have to get home to Jim and the kids. I wondered if they thought about me. Did Proctor get my voicemail? I miss my family so much. I couldn't stop thinking of them and how big of a hug I want to give all three. No matter how hard Jim was on me I would give everything just to feel the warmth of his embrace.

How big was this forest? I have been walking for what seemed like hours. The time moved with the sun. At least I wasn't going to get turned around if I just kept the sun to the back of me. Shouldn't that mean west is always behind me? The more I walked the more apparent it was how hungry I was getting. I only ever got to eat dinner with Victor and I was never able to have seconds. He always said he hated fat women and he needed to make sure I stayed skinny. I just kept walking til my legs gave out. The last thing I remember was a bright light flashing in my eyes as they closed shut from exhaustion.

Chapter 13
The Voicemail

Proctor hurried to the door of his father's house. Chadwick and Jim rushed to him from the barn they were working in. The worry on everyone's face was apparent.

"Listen to the voicemail" Proctor stated.

Jim and Chadwick listened with fear in their eyes. Regina was definitely in trouble. How were they going to find her? They hopped in Jim's truck and sped to the police station. It was a busy day and they could not get anyone's attention. Officer after officer was taking care of other inmates and files and they were getting pissed. Jim stood on a chair and yelled at everyone.

"I need an officer and I need an officer now!"

The station went quiet. The chief slammed his door open and asked who the hell was yelling. Jim stated he had information about his missing wife and no one will take the time to listen to him. The chief told the three men to come into his office.

"Who is this concerning?" The chief asked.

"It's my wife. She has been missing for months and I have filed a missing person report and everyone kept telling me she had run away. My son received a phone call this morning and she is in trouble." Jim explained to the chief.

The chief listened intently to the pleading of the voice.

"Do you recognize this number?" the chief asked.

"No. Not at all" said the men.

The chief paused for a minute and started typing rapidly on his computer. He ran the number through the database and couldn't find anything.

"I am going to call the phone company to see if we can ping the location where this number was last used but I am making no promises. The phone companies don't like to do anything without a warrant and we don't even have a name for a suspect. I want you all to go home and wait for my call" explained the chief.

They couldn't do anything else. They had nothing to go on. Where they lived, there were woods everywhere and hospitals all over. There was no narrowing it down. They drove back to Jim's in silence.

Chapter 14
Found

Something wet was upon my head. It was covering my eyes and felt so nice on my forehead. Afraid to open my eyes, I laid there for a few moments to enjoy the relaxation from the fight in the forest for so long. Even if I was back with Victor, I just felt solemn in that moment. I felt flannel on my arms and fleece on my legs. Fuzzy socks caressed my sore, swollen feet. I smell chicken soup and I want to say grilled cheese. The bed I was laying in definitely felt different than the one I had been chained to for the last few months. Perhaps Victor put me in a new room in his house, one that I couldn't escape from at all this time. At some point, I was going to have to open my eyes and face reality. This small amount of bliss will not last forever.

I brought my arm up slowly to my face. I could definitely feel the exhaustion deep in my muscles. I grabbed the wet thing off my face, which I now figured out was a wash rag, and slowly lifted it from my eyes. I didn't open my eyes right away. I felt a hand wrap around mine and I winced in fear. It was gentle and removed the rag from my grasp. I slowly opened one eye and was taken aback by a strange man's face in front of me. I had no idea who this man was. He was older. So many wrinkles defined the many years he had smiled. I looked into this man's eyes and there was this sweet, caring gleam and yet as I stared in disbelief, I noticed this deep pain in them. This man had to have been through so much in his life. I don't know what but I feel I am in a safe place.

"How are you feeling?" this man asked me.

"Where am I?" I stuttered.

"I found you in the woods, dirty and cold," he remarked. I picked you up and brought you into my home to warm you and get you fixed up.

I looked down and found a red plaid flannel buttoned up to my neck and red plaid fleece pajama pants. My socks looked to be from Christmas time and a fire was crackling beside me in the fireplace.

"What's your name?" I asked him.

"My name is Charlie. I am a widow of 10 years. I was married to my best friend for 59 years. She passed just shy of 3 months of our 60th anniversary." he replied without pause.

A tear showed through his bright green eyes. He proceeded to tell me his wife's name was Thelma, and how she always made sure he was on the path to success. He told me of his achievements, sacrifices, and failures. He spoke of love and loss. He was an officer in the Army during Vietnam. I couldn't do anything but stare into his eyes to try to see a glimpse of what his life was like through his eyes. For a brief moment, I forgot about my own trials. He was so expressive it gave me goosebumps. I knew he had to have seen the bruises on my wrists and ankles and my healing hand because he changed my clothes when he found me. And yet, he has not asked me once what happened. Of which I am thankful, but I now must tell my story. Charlie brought me tea from the kitchen and pulled up a rocking chair beside the bed and stated "when you're ready". He listened intently.

A knock on the door made me jolt. I jumped out of the bed making my cup of tea fly through the air and spilled onto the carpet. I crawled under the bed so fast I burned my knees on the rug. Charlie placed his index finger on his mouth and shushed me quietly. He threw on his plaid flannel very calmly and walked out of the room. The knocking happened again, this time a little harder and a little faster.

"I'm coming, I'm coming" I heard Charlie banter.

The lock clicked. The door squeaked open.

"What can I do for you, mister?" Charlie asked.

"I'm looking for my wife, she's beautiful and probably without shoes. She was diagnosed with dementia a few months ago and I had taken a nap and she accidentally went out of the front door alone. I believe she is lost and in danger." I knew that voice.

It was Victor no doubt. And he was making up a bullshit

storyline so it looks like I am the crazy one. I hope Charlie sees through his lies. Terrified, I backed as far as I could next to the wall.

"Can't say I have, sir." Charlie scratched his scruffy cheek. "Say, don't I know you? What's the name...Victor!" You live down the road. Charlie was saying these things loud enough so I could hear.

"Yes, that's me. I suppose I have seen you around a few times. You're alone, right? Widow?" Victor was prodding for information.

"Been gone 10 years. Now I just enjoy my time in solitude." Charlie said nonchalantly.

The next sentence I heard chilled me to the core. I felt so bad that I involved this amazingly sweet man into this horrifying situation.

"I noticed you have quite a few tea bags on your counter there for one person." Victor got very stern.

"I believe it's time for you to go now, Victor." Charlie stiffened. "Nothing you're looking for here boy. The door started to squeal shut.

BAM!

"I know you're here Regina!" Victor yelled in his pissed-off tone.

"Victor, you have to the count of three to get the hell out of my house and off of my property. Charlie meant business.

Those heavy footsteps made it to my door. The knob turned. I clenched my hands over my mouth to keep the screams inside me from getting out and actually making the sounds I so desperately want to make. I shut my eyes tight.

"AHHHH!" I yelped in terror.

Victor grabbed my ankles in complete brute force and dragged me out from under the bed. I watched Charlie wrap his arms around Victor's big masculine body to try to get him off of me and Victor elbowed him in the jaw and knocked his dainty body to the floor.

"Charlie! I'm so sorry!" I cried.

"Regina, I have no words for you. You broke my trust. And now you will suffer for the rest of your miserable, lonely, life." Victor stared into my soul with hatred.

It was almost like I actually caught a glimpse of hell's fiery rivers in those black holes of despair surrounded by the bloodshot white of his eyes. His left hand held onto my ankle as his right hand jerked into my throat. I couldn't breathe. The gasp of fear blew out of the bottom of my diaphragm. Victor just kept squeezing and squeezing. Darkness clouded my vision. It was like I was standing in a tunnel in a mountain where the only light was at the very end. I lost feeling in my legs and my arms. I was going limp.

POW! POW! POW!

Shots rang through my ears. I looked at Victor and his eyes were huge. It didn't occur to me what happened until Vic's hand let up off my neck and he fell forward, falling on top of me. All I could do was cry.

"It's okay, it's okay," Charlie said, trying to soothe me.

Charlie kicked Victor's limp body off of mine and pulled me into his arms. For being such a fragile-looking man he was incredibly strong. I just shrugged into his embrace. Then I cried, and I sobbed, and I couldn't stop thanking him.

"Let's go call your family," Charlie whispered in my ear.

Chapter 15
Phone Home

Jim, Proctor, and Chadwick sat around the kitchen table in silence. Jim made a hot pot of coffee and poured a cup for each of them. They were so lost in what they needed to do, that they did nothing. Jim tried to come up with something to say, but nothing came to mind. There was nothing he could say that would make this situation better. Jim's phone rang. All three men froze in fear. What if it was the police telling them they found her dead? What if it was just a telemarketer or a bill collector? Jim peaked. A number they didn't know. It wasn't an *877 number so maybe it was just a wrong number.

"Hello?" Jim whispered.

"JIM!" Regina cried through the phone.

Jim immediately broke into tears. It was Regina. His wife, his love, his children's mother, his best friend, and everything in between. The boys had never seen their father cry like that in their life. Maybe this really was a turning point for the family.

"Baby, where are you?" Jim pleaded. "I need you to come home. I need you. We need you."

All Regina could do was sob through the phone. She couldn't make out any words even though she tried so hard. Charlie gently took the phone out of her grasp and wrapped his arm around her shoulders.

"Hello, Jim. My name is Charlie. I found your wife passed out in the woods near my home. The police are on their way. She's been through an incredible amount, but she is safe now. "

Chapter 16
A Family Again

Pounding on the front door followed. Charlie went to release Regina from his hold but Regina didn't want to be left alone. She grabbed Charlie's hand and stared into his eyes. Charlie knew that look, so he enveloped her hand with his and led her to the front door. He slowly creaked the big block of wood open. Regina was shaking in her bones even though she knew the whole situation was over. She peaked through the sunlight to see two uniformed men standing there with their hands on their guns. Regina was so relieved.

"Police. Are there any weapons?" they stated.

"They're in the other room where I shot the bastard." Charlie snapped back.

"Put your hands up and slowly step back." The police meant business.

"This is Regina. She was kidnapped from a park and held against her will. We are not the enemy here." Charlie didn't like the way the police were treating us already.

"Regina. Where do I know that name..do you have a crazy husband and 2 very loud sons?" one officer asked.

Regina smirked slightly and nodded her head. That means they went to the police. They were looking for me, she thought. They actually cared.

"We are going to need to take you both down to the station to get your statements. " the police said as they made their way into the other room to peek at the scene.

"I will drive us. She has been through enough. She doesn't need to be put into the back of a police car for defending herself from this monster" Charlie wasn't letting me out of his sight.

The police nodded and told them to stay right behind his patrol car. At this time 3 other police cars showed up in the drive.

"We are calling your husband and sons to come down and meet us at the station," they told her. Regina was so elated to see her family.

She didn't care at all what had happened these past years, she just wanted her family together again. A family didn't have to be perfect, it just had to be their own. The drive seemed to take ages. As they went along she started to recognize her surroundings. She had actually only been a couple of miles away from the park this whole time. Which means she was only a couple miles from home the whole time. Regina didn't know how to feel about it. If she was only good with directions, maybe she could have been able to get home safe and earlier.

They pulled into the police station and immediately saw Jim's truck. Three men emerged and her face lit up brighter than the desert sun.

"My boys, my boys!" She screeched out.

She jumped out of Charlie's truck before it even came to a stop. She left the passenger door open and ran full force into Jim's embrace. He squeezed so hard and kissed her so passionately. Something he hadn't done in years. She felt so blessed. She took a second to hug her boys one by one.

"You got my voicemail?" Regina asked Proctor as she cupped his cheeks in her hands.

"Of course, mom. We have been together ever since waiting for you." Proctor replied.

Next, she took Chadwick's face in her palms.

"Oh Wicker. I have missed your handsome face." Regina stared into his eyes as she spoke.

Chadwick sort of melted. He was this strong 18-year-old man now that is living on his own and making a life for himself away from all of the bullshit. I couldn't blame him. Now, maybe things will be different. She hoped to

God with everything she had that things would be different from now on.

"Charlie!" Regina gasped.

She spun her head around but didn't see him. Regina started to panic. An officer opened the door to the station and waved them over. Jim grabbed her hand and wrapped his arm around her waist. They walked in perfect alignment with each other, step by step being the same. Like they had never been apart. Proctor walked in front of Regina and Jim and Chadwick walked behind them. Regina could feel the protection from her three favorite people.

As they walked through the doors of the station, Regina's eyes met with Charlie's. She smiled with relief in her eyes. Charlie laid his hand over his heart and started to tear up. He walked over to Regina and her boys, rather men now. He put his hand out to Jim first.

"Howdy, the name is Charlie," he stated and Jim grabbed his hand and shook it once, but did not let go.

They stared at each other for what seemed like ages.

"Thank you. Thank you for saving my wife." Jim said.

"You've got a very strong woman there Jim.

Don't let her go again." And with that Charlie let go of Jim's hand.

Proctor and Chadwick took turns shaking Charlie's hands until the officers came over. They told Regina and Charlie it was time to take statements. Jim went to follow, but Regina turned to him and laid her hand on his chest.

"I need to do this myself first." she looked him in the eyes. "I will be right back and then I am never leaving your side again."

Jim gently kissed her on her lips and nodded. Jim and the boys sat in the chairs right outside of the office where Regina was giving her statements. It took over an hour for her to give the police all of the details of this horror. She talked about the park and the deer. She told of the violence that ensued in Victor's home. The burned hand and the hospital trip. The infection that would scar her hand forever. The getaway and the woods. Then she told of Charlie rescuing her and saving her by shooting Victor as he pulled her from under the bed and strangled her until she thought she was releasing her last breath. She made sure to tell of every single instance that happened so that she knew for a fact that Charlie was not going to be in trouble for killing a dangerous man.

The door opened from the office, and Regina emerged. All three men stood up and wrapped their arms around Regina to give her solace. The officer told them they had enough information and that they could go home. Charlie came out of the office beside them. Regina looked worried for a minute thinking he was going to be arrested but the officer shook Charlie's hand and thanked him for saving Regina and for the bravery it took to save her a second time from a man that was out to kill. Regina jumped into his arms and hugged him tightly.

"I want you to be a part of our family. I know you have none now that your wife has passed and you have no kids." Regina told him.

"I would love that, Regina." Charlie smiled as he spoke.

Jim, Proctor, and Chadwick shook his hand. Charlie gave Regina his phone number and told her that when she was settled down and back in her routine to give him a call. He would always have the phone with him waiting for her call.

Chapter 17
The Bench

Regina and her family arrived home a short time later. They walked to the front door together. Regina stopped and knelt down. She placed her palm on their front door-step where a carpet lay that read " Welcome". She closed her eyes and breathed in the smells of their property. She could smell the flowers from her garden. She opened her eyes and glanced over to where she spent so many mornings tending her plants. It was in pristine condition. It almost looked better than when she was caring for it.

"I made sure I watered them every day and weeded them so that when you came home, you wouldn't be disappointed in me that your garden had wasted away." Jim expressed.

Regina smiled a big toothy grin. She squeezed Jim's hand in love. Proctor opened the door to their home, and she was hit with a lemon and bleach scent. She saw that someone had cleaned the entire home.

"I wanted to show you I was not going to be who I was before," Jim explained.

Jim, Proctor, and Chadwick proceeded to make a large feast for Regina to show appreciation and a step toward peace in the family. The rift from so many years of hatred and anger between everyone had lifted. It finally felt like home. None of the men asked Regina what she had gone through. They saw her hand and the bruises on her wrist. Her black eye and the bruise in the shape of a hand around her throat. They figured she would talk when she was ready. Until then, they just wanted to be the family they should have been all along.

They finished dinner. Regina thought it was the best meal she had ever had. The love she tasted within the food from the three was immaculate. They washed the dishes and put them away. They asked Regina not to lift a finger. No longer was she the person taking care of everyone else, they were going to take care of her. Jim asked the boys if they could hold the fort down because he wanted to take Regina up the hill. They nodded. Jim took Regina's hand in his and asked her to go on a walk with him. They walked past the garden and up a trail. She had always wanted to do this with Jim but it never happened.

As they came upon the top of the hill, Regina burst into tears. There sat a bench painted in her favorite plum color. A heart is etched into the wood with the letters "J" and "R" in it. The bench she had always told Jim she wanted.

"Chadwick and I built it and painted it together. I hope it is what you wanted." Jim said as he looked to the ground not knowing if he had failed her again.

"Oh Jim, it is perfect." Regina sobbed.

They embraced each other and for the first time and never the last, they sat and watched the sunset on their perfect bench. They were finally at peace.

Epilogue

There on that bench, Regina told the events of what happened that dreadful day she was kidnapped and everything in between, until she met them back at the police station. Jim sat tentatively without saying a word. His heart ached for his wife. He knew she did not deserve anything that had been thrown at her in the years they had been together. She would never tell her sons what happened so they didn't think ill of her for her weaknesses.

"I won't ever let you down again, honey," Jim said in a stern tone.

"I love you, Jim," Regina said and leaned in for a passionate kiss.

Days went past and Jim kept his word. He awoke with her every morning at 6 a.m. to make breakfast and help her tend her garden. A week after Regina arrived home, he remembered he had put all of his money into a last-ditch stock to save their finances. He walked into his office and peeked at his screen. Jim turned white as a sheet.

"Regina! Regina! Get in here!" he yelled so loud.

She didn't know what to think so she ran in shaking in worry.

"Look, baby. Look." Jim said as he pointed to the screen.

There on the screen was his stock account. It read $1.7 million and was rising.

"It's not about the money, I know, but we can save the house and the land and we can retire. We can be with each other every single minute for the rest of our lives. It was my last ditch effort to save us." Jim explained.

With that, they lived their lives in happiness. They were safe. They were together. Proctor and Chadwick moved back home. Jim bought them homes down the road from Jim and Regina's so that Regina could have her whole family together whenever she wanted. They would have Charlie over for Sunday dinner every week and go to lunch on Wednesdays. Jim spent every minute he could with Regina. He even went with her to the park on Saturdays and donned an apron that matched his wife's. It was their stand now, not just Regina's. She was no longer alone in her life.

The camera she had used that day she was kidnapped, got put up in the back closet of the home. She did not want to know if she ever snapped a shot of that deer. She had put the past behind her and all that was left was the nasty scar on her hand that she would eventually forget was there, in time.

Author
Morgan Plantz